# "JOHN AND OTHER STORIES"

Stories From George Coombs

Bloomington, IN     Milton Keynes, UK
authorHOUSE®

AuthorHouse™  
1663 Liberty Drive, Suite 200  
Bloomington, IN 47403  
www.authorhouse.com  
Phone: 1-800-839-8640  

AuthorHouse™ UK Ltd.  
500 Avebury Boulevard  
Central Milton Keynes, MK9 2BE  
www.authorhouse.co.uk  
Phone: 08001974150  

© 2007 George Coombs. All rights reserved.

No part of this book may be reproduced, stored in a retrieval system, or transmitted by any means without the written permission of the author.

First published by AuthorHouse     3/15/2007

ISBN: 978-1-4259-8919-4 (sc)

Printed in the United States of America  
Bloomington, Indiana

This book is printed on acid-free paper.

# John

Deep, piercing fear. Thoughts swirling like scattered autumn leaves. Where was he? Who was he? Did anyone actually care? Frail and helpless several strange lights seemed to glare him. He was flat and could only look up at a ceiling. A dull ache in his side. Mind hurt and fragmented. No linking or relating to his surroundings. A constantly flowing sea of voices. Busy, rushing activity. John felt he was in some sort of bed and his movement seemed restricted.

Pieces came together that had been savaged and torn apart. So, is this it? Was he now dead? In some kind of waiting area? Very little movement seemed possible and John wondered if he was in some way out of his body. He began to remember and in that remembering felt overwhelmed by a sense of betrayal. He longed to leave his present life. Yes, of course there was anger, also profound desperation and the suffering of a slow death inside. Screaming nobody wanted to hear. Need of freedom from the pain of life.

A longing for self-destruction had consumed him. No meaning or purpose, drowning in feelings of loss and betrayal. Constant offering of himself thrown back in his face. From the very edge of life he looked far outward. Before him the vast sea lay calm and still in late autumn light. Cool breeze disturbed the grass beneath his feet there on the high cliff just outside of town. One purpose only dominated his being there. A sturdy fence lined the cliff edge. John knew that suicide from this spot was by no means an uncommon occurrence; he felt nobody knew or cared where he was. It was like a numbing thrust that pierced his being.

Yes, there were things he was very ashamed of. Things about himself that nobody should ever know yet; what urged him there were very real feelings of rejection hurt and betrayal. Nobody could know them quite as he did. There was too an unbearable sense of isolation and profound loneliness. It was the only thing left to do yet; there was something that had stopped him. Slowly he left the cliff edge. On the way home he purchased many tablets.

Now, as he lay in this place desperate thoughts, feelings and memories gradually came together. John became aware of tubes emanating from various parts of his body. People in uniforms, men and women. Constant, seeming unending murmur of voices. John was in hospital. A young Jamaican nurse with a gentle voice asked –

"How ya doin' honey?"

"Alright.... I think" John told her. It was good to feel safe with someone. Now he as least knew he was alive and not dead. The nurse carried out his medical observations, she seemed so very genuine.

"You just lay back and take it easy" she said smiling "And hey, it'll all be Ok. Give it time, all will be well."

These were not just words and a nice bedside manner. John somehow sensed that she knew it and meant it.

"Will everything be alright?" he asked.

"Yes" she said kindly, then walked away.

John lay back and closed his eyes. Again the memories. More pieces in the complex jigsaw of his personhood.

John was at his desk staring at the tablets. There was an acceptance of what he felt he should do. Life had come apart six years ago when Mum died. So much of his wholeness as a person had died with her. Just a few months ago Dad had also passed on, Mum has passed away when she was seventy seven, she had known Dad since she was fourteen. John remembered all those years he has cared for his mother who was wheelchair disabled with arthritis. Throughout those years she had shown wonderful courage and good humour, she had a lovely smile and was always concerned for the welfare of others.

Various papers lay in a tidy pile in one corner. The telephone. Shelves of books above him. Books, knowledge and understanding had always mattered. Mum and Dad had been so proud of the family's only academic. Turning, he gazed out of the window. Late afternoon. The sky was slowly darkening. Branches of a nearby tree seemed to wave frantically and with desperation. Sense of gathering darkness all around him. John did not want to be a burden to anyone at all; he was not like that and never had been. This was it. This had to be the only way. John went to the kitchen for some water then began taking the tablets, a hundred and forty analgesics. Soon he would join his parents. More and more of him died inside. This would be the loss. Not actual death but what had become fragmented and died inside him while he yet lived. Loss of so much through loneliness. Isolation. Looking for real and meaningful relationships. Real meaning and purpose. There were things about him nobody would ever know. No trust of people allowing oneself to be vulnerable yet; is one not always vulnerable?

Movement. Porters and a Nurse were taking him to a ward. They passed along several corridors. All the time constant noise and movement. Then into a lift before arriving on the ward. Rush, noise and stress. The hospital was, like so many, grossly understaffed, under resourced and badly managed. He drifted into sleep. Opening his eyes he was on the ward and in bed, a bed he would constantly hear referred to as bed seven. It was early morning yet still the impression of everyone everywhere being just so busy. There seemed to be so much stress and pressure on the staff.

Memory. At his desk the feeling overwhelmed him. Gradually, a handful at a time, he swallowed every single one of the tablets washing them down with water. Thought and reason were numbed. Purpose, rescue could only be achieved by destroying himself. Refuge for John was death. In what seemed like a moment all the tablets were gone; he had taken the lot.

Some of the tubes had been removed from his body. An intravenous infusion was still in progress. John carefully eased himself up in bed and eat a light breakfast. Not steady. Not sure. Distance between him and his surroundings.

John knew and could certainly feel what he had done. He was taken over, a force; a sinister thinking energy had driven him to this. Taking a pencil, hands trembling slightly, he scribbled a quick note. It was done. Now the waiting. John felt a strange, almost frightening sort of calm acceptance of the situation; he put his new coat on and went out for a walk. There were many pubs in the area where he would be known. The nearest was just a few minutes away and he did not go in there very often. There could be a few people there who would know him, at least by sight. Whisky. John walked in, noise, music, loud uninhibited talking and laughter as well as heavy drinking. John ordered a double whisky.

"Goin' out?" someone asked

"Yes" John said thoughtfully, "I am"

The pub was very busy. Groups of people laughed and chattered all around him. Some knew him yet, a feeling of distance. Death is the final, inevitable journey in mortal life. Leaving of all kinds of sorrow and pain behind. Links with loss, with grief. What did it actually feel like? Not that anybody could really know or, if they did how exactly would they describe it? At times language was conspicuously inadequate. Killing of oneself. A definite feeling of betrayal.

Yes, there were people there who knew him but it was all so shallow, empty and superficial. To whom was he precious? Suicide means humanity's ultimate betrayal of itself. John drank the whisky quickly, he did not particularly like the taste and, infact, seldom drank spirits yet, it had to be done. He was starting to slip away. As a rule John would only ever go to a pub to be among people even the shallow, superficial and often very nasty people who used pubs so often to openly and blatantly deal in illicit drugs. Such, often was the pub population in the area

John got carefully off the stool by the bar and walked out into the cool evening air.

The overdose John had taken was a massive one. Something he gradually came to realise was that he had many real and very genuine friends. He actually was of value yet somehow he was unable to acknowledge this. Some friends had already been to the hospital to see him. Mary, John, Jayne and Mike who lined in a special way with that fateful night. There was a profoundly spiritually spiritual dimension that enriched their friendship with each other.

From the pub to the heavily populated street. The road was busy with traffic. Noise everywhere. A queue at the bus stop. All carried a feeling of distance. There was a sense of Mum and Dad. They were together now. End of all suffering and seperation. Together in all the sublime vastness of eternity. For as long as forever is. It was not the first time. John had walked this path before. When Mum passed on he just couldn't cope at first. They had become so close "travelling companions" and "special friends" Mum had often said. Some, then, had said he was "weak" he should "let her go" and "pull himself together" but then, as now, he was truly human. Part of the ever turning cycle of nature, frail like a lost leaf in autumn…John survived and was beside his mother at her funeral, now often, he would visit her grave with her there too in a very real spiritual sense.

John continued his slow walk along the street. Noise, cold, flashing lights all had the nature of fragmented perceptions and feelings. Increasing sense of distance from his surroundings. A sense of Mum and Dad. Every so often he tingled.

There was the wanting, longing to be rid of the pain, isolation and betrayal that had eaten into his life like a malignant disease.

"Hi John"

It was Mike. A good kind man john had known for some time. John faintly felt like telling Mike what he had done. No, he couldn't. Enough was enough. Truths existed about him that nobody could ever know. Truths concerning hurt, the person he was and death inside. John returned his greeting and enquired after Mike's family who he also knew well.

"They're just fine thanks mate" said Mike "Where ya doin'?

"O…just out for a bit of a walk…. A breath of fresh air."

"You look tired ya know mate? Mike told him "Very tired"

"I am"

John certainly was very tired. He did want that breath of fresh air yet only if it might be breathed in another life. He just could not stand it any more. Cries and screams had vanished into the emptiness of life. They parted. John walked on until he came to a seat; he sat down longing to sleep forever. He was slipping away, legs, arms, hands, were numb, slow, shallow breathing…first real glimmerings of fear….

The pace on the ward was hectic. Some of the patients were clearly in a critical. John had a quick wash and sat quietly by his bed, bed seven. Many thoughts and concerns crowded into his mind. He was not dead so where now in his life? What direction and, why had his attempt not actually worked? A Doctor had told John that his liver was damaged. People had already said he should try and give up alcohol; he never had actually drank all that much but, for several reasons keeping away from pubs could well be a good thing. It was only the terrible, penetrating sense of loneliness he had known that caused him to drink at all. Loneliness and the deep, inner questions it inevitably poses. Most of the people he had known from pubs were not nice at all but there were a few welcome exceptions to this.

Mum's passing on had devastated him. His constant companion and very special friend was gone. They had become very close during those years he cared for her. Every morning they met, John helped Mum with everything, they had breakfast then would go out together shopping and, often, they would have a meal together and it was a lovely time for which John's mother was always so very grateful and appreciative. So many wonderful memories. John did all her treatment and, using his hands and knowledge of oils skilfully, he helped and brought his mother considerable relief. In carrying out her treatment there developed a special love between them and their hearts merged in a ministry of touching and holding.

After Mum passed a lot of people just did not understand in any way yet, there were the dear people who accepted him jus as he was in this time of sorrow and grieving. John needed this acceptance and the quality of healing that it held. There were so many tears when Mum passed on leaving him with a screaming emptiness, a profound sense of loss and unbearable loneliness. They were indeed special friends and their friendship held a clear spiritual quality.

One day, shortly after the passing, John happened to go into the pub around the corner shortly after it opened. From time to time he would take Mum in there.

John had a beer and Mum had ginger wine. People working there were always kind and helpful and one special person was Liz.

"Hiya" Liz said cheerfully as he walked in.

"Hi Liz" John replied quietly.

Liz had a warm, caring nature and a lovely smile; she originally came from Liverpool where her father worked as a Prison Officer but she had been in john's area for some time. They knew each other well and had become friends, sensing something was wrong Liz asked –

"How's Mum?"

John burst into frantic weeping. Liz gently led him to a seat and sat with him. Tears flooded his face. No other customers were there and the manager, Phil, told Liz to stay with John; she held him quietly.

"I'm so sorry Liz" John told her"

"Nothing to be sorry for, it's alright. I'm here my love; you just let it all out. It's fine. I'm here; we're all here for you. Nothing to be sorry for at all."

It was good to feel safe and cared for. Liz had such kind and wonderful qualities. One of the others brought him a cup of coffee. For a few moments no sound as John gladly felt the relief of Liz holding him. The crying eased. There was tightness in his chest. Looking through tears Liz was still there, smiling she kissed him gently, a lovely cool and calm feeling. The tightness eased.

"I know" she said quietly "And I know your Mum was so very lucky to have such a loyal and devoted son with special skills and qualities, she was proud and in her closeness and love I know she still is proud and John…"

"..Yes"

John looked at her.

"I'm very proud of you too."

They embraced. John was thankful for a real friend and the loving refuge of her holding. In her quiet arms he was safe. Some moments of beautiful silence between them and then, John kissed her gently on the forehead and left.

"Hello there"

A hand on his shoulder. John slowly opened his eyes, he was still linked to the memory of Liz and wanted to see her there. It turned out to be the nice lady who took orders for meals; she noted John's requirements then left. After a few moments a male nurse came and told John a psychiatrist would be coming to see him later in the day. This came as no real surprise. During the initial period following Mum's passing John had also tried to end his life. Now, a few years later, another attempt and by far the most serious one. This time there were certain other matters involved like guilt, shame and confusion yet there were also the clear common denominators of loneliness and a feeling of betrayal. John knew what they felt like and their wounds were a constant pain to him.

John knew he was someone who needed a sense of meaningful community. Not just people coming together and being linked by superficial self-centeredness. But truthful and meaningful belonging where he felt accepted just as he was.

Recovery was slow following Mum's death. There was this void, this hurting emptiness. Mum had been his close and constant companion. They were, as she had always said, such 'special friends.' John could feel she was at peace and happy now and he could often sense her with him. So many treasured memories of things only he and his mother would ever know. John had made an attempt on his life then, as he no longer had a life to live. At that time, as now, an overdose of tablets had taken him into hospital. Then, as now, he had been referred to a psychiatrist.

John opened his eyes. Seemingly endless activity in the ward; he read for a while then walked slowly along a corridor pausing every so often to gaze from a window at the world outside. The area where he found himself situated was on an upper floor of a large modern building. From this height he could rest his eyes on the sea, which he and Mum had always loved, and the Gulls gliding gracefully in the wind, floating with outstretched wings as if welcoming nature and life with its often seemingly endless buffeting of frail human beings. Thoughts of ending returned, his mind was still fragmented and in pain. Again he remembered Liz and smiled.

"You look happy"

John turned. It was the young Jamaican nurse from 'A and E.' such a very kind person with a pleasant and welcoming smile.

"Good" said John "I was just remembering a very special friend from way back."

"Lovely" she said " I helped look after you on A and E when you were first brought in."

" I remember you"

"I've just finished and I thought I'd pop round, I wanted to know how you were getting on."

"How very kind of you" John told her "Well, I think I'm feeling a good deal better in myself but, I've got a whole load of stuff to sort out."

"Sure, I understand"

After a pause she told him –

"We thought we were going to loose you at one point."

"Was I that bad then?"

"You sure were honey, we had you on a respirator and everything, it was real touch and go for a while, you'd taken one massive overdose."

John felt touched by her concern. Such a sincere person with a lovely smile. A stranger who was actually concerned for him.

"Well, I must go now, you take care honey, bye"

"Bye" said John "And…Thankyou so much."

The nurse smiled, winked at him and walked away. John returned to looking out of the window. Still the Gulls calling across the vast, pigeon grey sky. A male nurse from the ward came and told him a psychiatrist would come and see him during that evening and that Mike was coming during the afternoon. It would be good to see Mike again; he had been friends with him and his wife Jayne for a long time. Gradually he was acknowledging that he was actually special to some people.

There were too, those whose cruelty and betrayal had deeply disturbed him. They caused him to feel of no value; afraid to take the risk of being open and vulnerable, slowly he returned to the ward, sat by his bed and read for a while.

Reading was vital for John; he loved learning and the written word and would spend many hours searching for wisdom and knowledge. By profession he was a qualified librarian and he also held a humanities degree, he worked for the local university. None of the people he worked with, and among, knew the real John. Relationships, though often pleasant were essentially superficial. There were some very nice, pleasant acquaintances but certainly no real friends. John knew he was fortunate in having a secure, reasonably salaried job yet; he had very deep rooted inner needs among them that of being accepted just as he was. Not just for his academic and librarianship skills but with his faults, failings and mistakes.

The book he was reading and, one that he often dipped into was a series of meditations by a great Chinese scholar of the past known as Chiang Yee. John knew his work well and had often been moved by his meditations that were so gentle, sensitive and profound. One captivated his attention; the word seemed so comforting, peaceful and somehow enabled him to be in a safe and special present moment.

> 'My child, I offer a book and a rose. Take the book and may you write on its pages words of light and truth. Receive what is offered gently and allow the pages to teach, to guide and to comfort. The book my child is the book of your life, the empty pages are waiting for you. What treasure is to be found in space and emptiness where I can await the fullness of wisdom, knowledge and love.
>
> The rose is beauty and stands by the book in clear water. Its petals open to light, it waits in all its natural

joy. The rose is life itself; it has beauty, also thorns and softness. Light and shadow. They walk together. Here within your grasp is simple wisdom that will take you on to deeper understanding. Words of light rest among the rose petals. Find beauty, joy and peace. The book is indeed yours yet write in it one page at a time. All that is needed is in the rose, it is the glory of creation as, indeed, you were borne to be. The book is your book of life; write other names as you are led by the spirit so to do. Write all that you learn. As you journey through the pages, which are your pilgrimage on earth, be open to light as the rose is open. Live one moment at a time as you turn the pages one at a time then you will never overlook the waiting treasures that are all around you.

Peace, love and rest are here and waiting. So often one can turn so many pages at once that one sees nothing and learns nothing. If you seek one-ness you will indeed find one-ness, by seeking peace and light one not only finds them but can share them with others until, on the final page you share that life is eternal and love in wisdom and truth will never pass away. Be always of good courage, a wise heart and a quiet time and all in the healing fullness of time will be well.

My Blessing<br>Chiang Yee'

There was always his blessing at the end, here were words and thinking that John could relate to; he was searching and here, in this wise and sensitive thinker he felt he had a gentle companion on the way. A wise and noble friend,

"Hello me old mate"

John looked up. It was always good to be with him but even more so now. Mike knew everything and John was glad that he did. They greeted each other warmly and John enquired after Jayne.

"She's just fine" said Mike "Sends her love to you and hopes to pop up to see you soon. Kids are fine too and all your friends from Church send their love and assure you of their ongoing prayers and concern."

"Thankyou Mike" said John quietly "That's so good to know"

Mike, ever kind and thoughtful had a few books for him, fruit and a newspaper. If ever there was someone who was welcome to know everything it was Mike. They had been firm friends since first meeting at a Church near to where John lived. There, and in his work with a local charity helping vulnerable people mike had often been glad of John's knowledge and academic skills.

"So how's it going?" Mike asked

A moment's hesitation

"Okay…. I think"

A calm, gathering silence between them.

"Try not to worry mate" Mike told him quietly "We're all here with you, praying for you and here to help and stand by you."

John felt deeply touched. Gradually he had warmed to the idea of prayer. It wasn't just words into empty air but actually talking to a divine person, the creator of everything. It was talking to God as a friend. Not just in a sort of academic sense but person to person.

"You're all so great" he told mike with feeling

"Well, it's what being real friends is all about" said Mike "You've been a great friend to so many John, perhaps without realizing it and, of course, Jesus called his disciples friends as you know."

"Yes, and Abraham was the friend of God."

"Spot on as always" Mike declared, then asked –

"Are you at least fairly comfy here mate?"

"Yeah" said John, its loads better than police custody anyway, "Couldn't be worse, I don't wonder there's so much self harm and suicide in custody."

"As bad as that you feel then"

"Without doubt Mike

From their own perspectives neither man was impressed with the "system" in England. They had definite, sustainable views as to who were the real criminals. They both felt that the so-called justice system and its enforcers were a means of securing upper class interest and perpetuating class conflict.

In his undergraduate days John had been politically active, attending demonstrations and had had several articles in printed in various student publications. Mike felt he was engaging with many of the repercussions of living in a deeply divided and unequal society in his work among the vulnerable. Meaningless duress and deprivation achieved nothing at all but the embitterment and dehumanisation the many whose desperate cries for help the powerful, devious and selfish found it easier to ignore.

The "system" protected the powerful and functioned as a result of oppression and fear. As he moved on John knew he would take with him a deeper understanding of why suicide and self harm in custody were so common and why the so called "precautions" regarding this were of no effect and constituted mindless ignorance and stupidity.

Put simply, it is the pain of feeling so much inside you die and often die in private agony. In modern times Magistrates, who are largely drawn from the rich and powerful, are unsalaried and this is just as well as they actually made no genuine contribution to a safer or more morally responsible society at all. John knew of a nineteenth century magistrate who had described his function as "the dirtiest job on earth" and is it any wonder?

In his spare time John wrote poetry, he had composed one concerning his experience in custody and showed it to his friend –

<u>From A Cell</u>
Still, deep in want,
Prisoner, fragmented mind
Trembling with sound of
Heavy door closing, looking

Then, roughly
Taken manacled
Labelled "criminal"
Never any listening

To cry for help.
Barren room,
No benefit of silence
Or peace, noise of

Pain from the hurt self
Yet, even here one
Can know mystery of
Holy holding
Feeling even here
Finder of the lost
Find me, tell me
"You are precious in my sight"

Crime is a mountain
Prayer and love can climb.
Crime is pain leading to pain,
Desperate cycle of agony.

Crime is a path lined
With tangled forests, a
First real step waits like a frightened child,
Those who do not seek do not find.

"Its' great John" said Mike "Makes you think"

"Good" said John "And that's the very thing we don't do all that often these days."

"So what's the next step as far as the hospital are concerned?"

"I'm seeing a psychiatrist a bit later on"

"How d'you feel about that?"

"Well…" John began hesitantly "It'll do no harm I suppose"

A moment of gathering silence. Each man knew the other well. John was only too well aware that he had to move on. There was this need for some guidance and clear seeing. Mike knew how deep thinking, widely read and learned John was.

"Are you worried about it?"

"Uneasy" John admitted "I try to pray Mike…I do try…but…"

"I know mate…"and I know Jesus is real and close to you"

"I talk to him"

"Good, and he hears you"

Mike was well aware of the problems and deep needs that John had confided to him. Noticing the book of meditations by Chiang Yee he browsed through its pages.

It does help" John told him "Gets me thinking, he talks about Jesus and religion quite a lot."

John paused for a while in deep thought. Silence between them. This was one area among many that they shared in common. A love of silence.

"I've seen a psychiatrist before"

"Yes, I know"

"Not a lot of help to be honest. Seemed to go round in circles, no helpful tablets, treatment or anything." Some rather vague talk of psychotherapy but I never heard anything more. Long waiting list or something. All the usual excuses. Mike I need help now."

"I know mate, " said Mike quietly "All your friends are here for you"

"Thanks" said John "I' so fortunate, I actually am, to have real friends."

"Well mate, you're a person whose precious in God's sight, and for us all who know you, you're a person of great value and worth."

John felt moved. The words had a lovely comforting vibration that moved his entire being. They spoke briefly about the whole idea of mental illness. Could this be some kind of social construction? Or perhaps the different parts of the self coming to the surface depending on our past experiences of life, where we are, who we are with etc. Was it, like 'crime' actually a somewhat vague term used by the powerful to label the vulnerable? Who are the actual victims? How many questions seek answers in real community? In what sense do we belong to each other? Mike glanced at his watch –

"Well, I have to go for now mate" he said

"Ok"

In a few moments of quietness Mike prayed for John then left. Within himself John was feeling calmer and more focused. Progress. Yes, it was actually possible to be glad that one was alive. It was possible to love and treasure yourself so that you could love and treasure others yet, also, there was a deep spiritual love that could ease the burden of guilt, the almost paralysing fear of discovery. John knew that the Bible spoke about the body as being a temple. A place of all that is loving, holy, pure and transcendent. Deeply felt forgiveness could be a real human experience; knowing that the secrets of one's past were not only forgiven but were forgotten. A man was approaching his bed; he was smartly dressed in a dark grey suit, black tie and white shirt. Under one of his arms he carried some case notes.

"Mrs Brown?" A quiet voice

"Yes, I am"

"I'm Doctor Richard Clark from the district mental health team"

"Pleased to meet you"

"And you"

They shook hands, he sat on the bed. Already, John was feeling a little apprehensive. How far would he probe? How much could he tell him?

"How are you feeling now? The Doctor asked

"Well, not to bad I suppose"

They began to talk about the overdose and exactly why John had tried to end his life. John spoke quietly and hesitantly. He was not comfortable talking about something like this, with its underlying implications, with someone he didn't know even if he was a Doctor. How do you bring yourself to talk about that which nobody but you would ever understand? The Doctor commented on how massive the overdose was. As if John actually needed to be told this? On that decisive night there certainly were a great many tablets. The deep longing was to be free from an existence that had inflicted such intense feelings of isolation on him especially since the passing of his mother. At times John felt is visitor seemed flippant and careless.

"Exactly what kind of help do you think you need Mr. Brown?"

John knew from previous experiences that this was frequently asked though occasionally phrased slightly differently. John always found it distressing. There was a lot he would have to face including the conflict with the authorities, notably the Police who had been so blind, careless and deeply damaging to all concerned.

"How the hell do you expect me to answer that?" he asked desperately

"Ok"

"I needed to die, I couldn't cope with such awful and horrid betrayal, the lies from a person who had asked for my help."

An uneasy silence between them. He seemed to be constantly returning to questions around why John felt he had to do what he'd done including why he had tried to kill himself. It all felt so pointless. After a while Doctor Clarke said he would arrange for a follow up out patients appointment to be sent to John then, he left.

John needed peace. There just had to be a way forward and one that grew from deep peace within himself. What was needed was a healing light to reach his spirit and for what had died inside him to be found and be borne again. John felt like a walk; he left the ward and strolled along the lift that took him to the next floor down where the hospital chapel was situated. John found it to be a tranquil and welcoming place. There was a modest altar and some beautiful stained glass windows. An open Bible rested on the Lectern. John sat quietly by a window that displayed Christ as 'The Light Of The World.'

It was so good to have some space and quiet. John gently closed his eyes. Who could ever understand his deep longings? Mike and he had often shared about spiritual matters and the person and teachings of Jesus. John turned and looked at the window behind him; light came through and in the gently coloured air John felt a welcome sense of peace and calm. In his own personal way John had given himself to Christ. Again he became aware that since the crisis of Mum's passing, and now, there actually were some wonderful people around. It became all the more clear that just as he was he could know himself as a person others loved and valued.

There, in the quiet, he remembered Mum and all they had shared together, laughter, pain and tears. What particularly came to mind was the park near where they had lived, Mum always enjoyed going their with John, feeding the pigeons and squirrels, seeing the crocuses when they were in bloom and in Autumn when the trees were bare and there were carpets of leaves everywhere she still loved it as did John himself. A poem he had written, linked to this period, came to mind.

<u>Again</u>

Again,
Sense of desolation,
Frost clings to grass,
Veins fragile leaves
Gives a sense of malignancy,
Choking of life,
Winter sun far away.
Heart and mind
Drift like a cold wind
To mystery of suffering.
All creation seemed pained
And you dearest Mum, why?
Your bones are delicate
As winter trees
Your pain tears me apart,
We look at the winter sun
And know even now there is light

Serving Mum, particularly with the skilled use of his hands and knowledge of things like Aromatherapy had meant a lot to him. Mum had always loved Lavender and John was never short of that also, his knowledge of Accupressure, massage and contact therapy brought her real relief from pain and she was always so very kind and appreciative of him. John would always be the first to acknowledge that during those years Mum gave him so very much.

Once again, John closed his eyes allowing himself to focus on his breathing. Gradually, his mind became quiet. A significant element of his academic work had been in the area of religious studies and he had wide knowledge and some practical experience of some years standing. John had once met a kind Buddhist monk who had taught him a simple and particularly practical meditation technique known as 'The Mindfulness of Breathing.' It helped. Opening his eyes John looked around; he rested on the window behind the altar showing a figure of Christ holding a young lamb. Here too light passed through the pane. John could feel a lovely sense of compassion from the picture; a calm which seemed to gather him into itself.

The Christ figure had wise, kind and yet penetrating eyes. The lamb that was lost had been found and seemed calm and peaceful in the safe refuge of the arms of Jesus. A profound simplicity. Still there was nobody in the chapel and it was a lovely space for him to just be. Somewhere, he couldn't just remember where, he had read of the pillars of the temple standing apart and the strings of a harp being apart though they quivered with the same music. Was this what Chiang Yee had called 'The Way Of the Wise Heart?' The finding of wisdom and meaningful knowledge and awareness in all that is simple and uncomplicated. John had not brought the book with him but could remember a meditation that began by asking, "Where is the way of the wise heart?" one of the answers to this was given as "Where there is inner peace and going forward on a path of learning and growth."

John felt he was desperately seeking that path yet, the way felt obscured by all the anxiety and the conflict within him. The path did need to be walked yet he could not walk it alone. Chiang Yee had often wisely said that on the path there were many shadows. They were kind and friendly teachers who one must learn to allow to teach. Closing his eyes he remembered words of this great Chinese sage whose thought he knew so very well. It seemed he could almost here him –

'Where is the holy quiet of strangers?

Hear it in space all around you.

Find it in stillness and seeking of wisdom and knowledge.

Quiet strangers only come when invited, will give to others a truly great gift, that of silence and space. In this space feel the gently vibration of eternity opening the way to wise ones, clear seeing angels. Allow time for you. Holy quiet is all around you. Look among strangers. Those who are near to you. Allow those with gentle, quiet vibrations to come. Those who give honour respect and indeed love. They also give the gift of space. They do not intrude. There is a door to peace with oneself. The handle is on the inside. Light, joy and wisdom are on the outside; only you yourself may welcome them in.

My Blessing

Chiang Yee

John felt calmer now and could recall Mike saying God would never allow what he could not use; he glanced at his watch. Soon, the evening meal would be brought to the ward. The colour, silence and space just to be were true nurturing friends. Quietly, and with a sense of gratitude he got up and left.

The ward routine varied very little from day to day. The beds were all numbers and John knew his was number seven. From time to time he had been a little disturbed to notice to notice that meals, medications etc. were directed to a number rather than a name and, sure enough, his evening meal came to 'bed seven.'

When he had eaten John sat quietly by his bed. After a little while he read some more from Chiang Yee then dipped into a Bible he had found in his locker; he did, of course know the Bible well and had several favourite passages.

"Hello there John"

John looked up. It was the Chaplain who he had met before since he had been in hospital. Reverend Keith Ellis seemed a kind and gentle man and John could sense he was safe with him.

"Hello" said John "It's nice to see you again"

"How are things going?"

"Well…not too bad, I suppose" John told him I saw a psychiatrist today and a friend has been who may come again this evening."

"O that's good, I'm glad to know you've got people supporting you at this time"

"I'm so fortunate" John said "And very privileged"

The Chaplain smiled. A moment of quiet between them.

"It shows you are valued" he said "And you are valued John, I do believe that"

"It's wonderful" said John smiling "You know, I feel I can actually believe that and it feels so good."

"And you are precious in the sight of God also"

"Wow" said john after a while.

There was, even with all his distress, a sense of real peace feeling like soft, comforting arms as it held him. John could actually know he was valued and loved as a real human being with all his frailty and vulnerability and even with the dark and secret places in his heart. The Chaplain saw the Chiang Yee book and glanced through it. John noticed his concentration and deep interest.

"I've heard of him" he told John "And I've read odd things yet…he paused "I don't think I've ever actually read his meditations before. Listen to this John, I think its wonderful –

> "Where is the way of the wise heart? Where droplets of rain glisten on a pink rose. Where there is inner peace and goin forward on a path of learning and growth. The wise heart lives in one moment at a time, is fully with each moment and mindful of the way things are. Along any path there are shadows dear one; they are your teachers who one need to allow to teach. They are the wise ones, the clear seeing light bringers, look for them for they are all around you and your dear ones at all times. The wise heart pulsates in all that is simple and uncomplicated. All that is close and gentle. Peace with yourself my dear one comes as one truly lives on moment at a time. Be in the now, listen to yourself.

Listen to the quiet voice of the angel within you who shines and longs to fill you with light. Go to that angel, for the angel waits for you to move on and learn from the shadows of the past. All the hurt from the past can be healed. Reach out to those you know only God could have sent to you. Truly, you know who they are. Allow the angel within you to show you the wisdom of forgiveness of others and, my child, yourself. Allow the wise heart to show you all you need to see. You are so loved in all your frailty, you are so special and precious. Allow the angel within you who embodies all your natural wisdom to shine in all area of your life as you journey on in purity and in peace.

My Blessing

Chiang Yee"

The Chaplain commented on his repetition of the word allow.

"Perhaps we need to consider" he said " How our lives are not as we would like because we do not allow them to be" he paused "And, I suppose allowing will always create a certain vulnerability."

"Yes" said John "I see what you mean, I know his work well and here's a wisdom I can very much relate to yet, there is always something new one can pick up."

In his quiet moments John had come to appreciate the Bible in a new and deeper way. They spoke about this for a while then the

*John and Other Stories*

Chaplain drew the curtains around John's bed. They shared 'The Lord Prayer' together then Keith Ellis prayed for John laying hands on him. Opening the curtains he left calmly and quietly as he had come. It was a pure light that was became brighter. John was, actually, precious and special. Life could be worth living. All he wanted to do was to be quiet and still. Yet there was the noise inside him.

Alone again. This could be when it became so very hard. Even when he was among people he knew, albeit at a very superficial level John often felt painfully wounded by loneliness, isolation, fear, a sense of distance between him and others. There was a dread of vulnerability and being hurt. Yet, a time of great personal crisis like this showed him the precious jewel of friendship, people who were near and who honestly cared and were concerned for him.

The Bible was near to him on his bed. John turned to the twenty third psalm 'The Lord Is My Shepherd', the passage "...even though I walk through the valley of the shadow' touched him and the words "...thou art with me." No indication of even a possibility that one might not walk through a personal valley of the shadow yet a person need not be alone. Shadows have many different forms, they had lengthened across his life yet, in such a valley it is possible and indeed necessary to allow the shadows to become teachers and friends. A person had to be open and receptive to love and acceptance yet also the ever present risks attached to vulnerability. Chiang Yee had said light and shadow walk hand in hand through life, how very true John knew this to be, he closed the Bible and put it down.

"Hello mate"

John welcomed the voice into his silence and space. It was Mike and Jayne was with him.

John got up and shook his hand warmly. Jayne brought him a lovely smile and a hug. It was good to be with them again and feel the comforting vibration of their friendship; good to feel so safe, accepted and indeed, loved. Jayne was just a little taller than Mike, tall, thin and had shoulder length hair.

"Is it very cold out? John asked.

"Sure is" Jayne told him as she briskly rubbed her hands together.

Removing coats, gloves and scarves they sat together on John's bed. John briefly recounted how he had spent the day and what he had been reading.

"Chiang Yee must have been a very wise and learned man" Mike said "And he comes over as very kind as well."

"That's good," said Jayne smiling

"And isn't the Bible an absolute treasure? I don't think I've ever really appreciated it in the way I do now even though I knew it so well. Its kind of like coming to it for the first time."

"I know just what you mean," Jayne told him "So what have you been reading from the Bible my little honey bunch?"

John smiled and felt happy inside. Jayne was a very special person and she often called him that; he shared with them his reading of the twenty third psalm and how this had once been his solo many years ago when he was a Church of England choirboy.

"Those were the days y'know" John said "Yours truly as a sweet, angelic, innocent

Church of England choirboy."

"Angelic?" asked Mike grinning "What you? Yeah, I bet"

"I was" John retorted smiling "I just can't think why nobody believes it"

"How often did your halo honey bunch?" Jayne asked grinning

"Well…." John began

"Come on" Jayne teased him "How often?"

"Well…actually…all the time my dear"

They laughed. John felt good; it was a relief to laugh and to be able to laugh with friends and to laugh at himself. It was good to feel the lightness between them.

"Heard how much longer you'll be here?" Mike asked

"Well, not for certain no, but I've picked up the odd hint that it might not be for much longer at all."

"How d'you feel about that mate?"

"A bit better Mike yet, kind of muddled and confused about things"

"That's understandable honey bunch; don't worry about it too much" Jayne told him and gently held hid hand.

A quietness came to him. John felt so safe and comforted. Such wonderful and real spiritual friends. Jayne's soft hand felt so safe. John could feel the gentle message of love and peace.

"Well, I guess we must think about going" Mike declared with a sigh.

"Okay"

They shared a time of meaningful prayer together then Mike and Jayne quietly left.

John returned to his reading of the twenty third psalm with its message of a kind shepherd seeking, finding and gently loving the sheep lost in the valley of the shadow. It spoke so clearly to him of the blessing of belonging.

"Well, how are you getting' on mate" asked a deep voice with laboured breathing.

John looked up. It was the man from the bed next to him, bed eight who had a long standing problem with his breathing. Ever since his admission to hospital John had not interacted all that much with other patients, he just didn't feel up to it, and he had only ever shared the occasional word with this man.

"Well, not too bad I suppose" John said "I may be discharged from here soon."

"Ok, good for you"

"And how about you?"

"Well there's some improvement from when I first came in I think. I've had this wretched thing with my chest for ages and it gets me down a bit sometimes. I had to take an early retirement because of it."

"What sort of work did you do?"

"Well, I've done loads of things but for ten years I owned and managed a second hand bookshop in Brighton."

"Sounds interesting" John said and went on to talk a little about his profession.

"Well, you'd 'ave liked my shop" he said "There was old books on every subject under the sun " – he became gripped by a coughing spasm and sat on John's bed for a while – "Sorry about that" he said as it eased "God, it does get me down."

"I'm sure"

"My dear wife's wonderful. I don't know how she copes with me sometimes, she's an angel."

"That's good to hear" said John

Normally he liked his own space and would not let other people reach him easily. Someone wanted to talk with him now and he found that he not only could listen but that he wanted to; he also felt his own lack of a lifetime companion.

"Is your wife in good health?"

"Yes thanks, she is, remarkable so" he said, "Well, I'm goin' to the day room to watch telly for a bit, you comin'?"

"Might do later on," John said

"Okay, cheers"

"Bye"

The man waked slowly away. John returned to the Bible and the words of the twenty third psalm. Again he took refuge in the comforting image of this shepherd walking beside him through the valley of the shadow. The idea of a table being set "…in the presence of my enemies" was also meaningful. There was a clear change in metaphor from a shepherd to a bounteous host; it would be safe from his enemies because eating at the host's table, he knew, signified being under his protection. Without doubt John had enemies and he had so often felt himself to be in the valley of the shadow especially since his mother had passed on. All through her final years of life John had cared for her and been at her side; he particularly remembered her last day, the collapse, going with her to the hospital, the same hospital he was in now, and her passing on to the next life.

This image of the shepherd also helped him feel Jesus the good shepherd living and walking in Mike, Jayne and the others who were caring for him and supporting him through this threatening and distressing period of his life. Light, he just wanted light to illumine the dark places within him and real spiritual wisdom for all the devastating loneliness he had often felt. John longed for peace, again he thought of Chiang Yee and the meditation that began with a question –

> 'Dear one, why are you here? Simply to learn, to love and to be loved. You have come from spirit, you will return to spirit. For this time of earth plane pilgrimage your spirit resides in an earthly body. So be aware of being human and frail and with that awareness be open to light coming from spiritual sources, light of love and

of truth. There will be illness, shadow, passing of life to higher life but be sure, you were born for this time when your light must shine forth – your dear one so very ill you feel for them, you will do as they are part of you and in being their loved companion you will journey together before the outcome is known, your loved one is in the hands of God and so are you my precious soul. Never doubt comfort comes in many forms, the kind smile, the gentle touch. The ministry of just being there. All you can offer is yourself. Put yourself in the hands of God who, in time gathers flowers from his garden. So, in your own human way and with awareness of how precious you are bring your sick one to the holy light, offer the longings of your heart, know angels, helpers, wise ones are all around you, you are never alone, trust that in the fullness of time children will dance in the streets of Zion, no more pain or suffering, all things will be well.

My Blessing<br>Chiang Yee

John was feeling increasingly tired, he lay on his bed and drifted away into sleep…

…Out of the door to be greeted by waiting cold air. Early morning, a sprinkling of bird songs and light gradually filling the sky. Deserted streets, a sense of quiet holiness as in an empty Church. A man with a feeling of calm and serenity about him walked toward John.

"Hello" he said softly and bowed slightly, John returned his greeting.

Walking quietly and slowly the man came near. John noticed a distinctly oriental look about him. The morning was becoming brighter.

"Peace is so very near friend" he said, "Peace waits like a lost and seeking child, longing to hold you, to be loved by you."

"But…where is this…child?"

"Deep within yourself…shining from the forest of shadows"

A quiet moment. John somehow felt he knew this man and could trust him.

" Yes, you do know me" the man affirmed smiling" I am Chiang Yee"

Beautiful white light around him. John could se a child running on ahead. He followed entering unending light…a voice said…

"I am the light of the world"

John knew all the colours of the rainbow were to be found in white. Still he walked on. Many friends from the past, even going back to school days, met him. Mum was there looking radiant, young and lovely. Dad was there too and they both rushed forward to welcome him. All was peace, joy, love and unending light…

… In the hospital ward Doctors and Nurses were around bed seven, the chaplain was there, the curtains were drawn….     - George Coombs

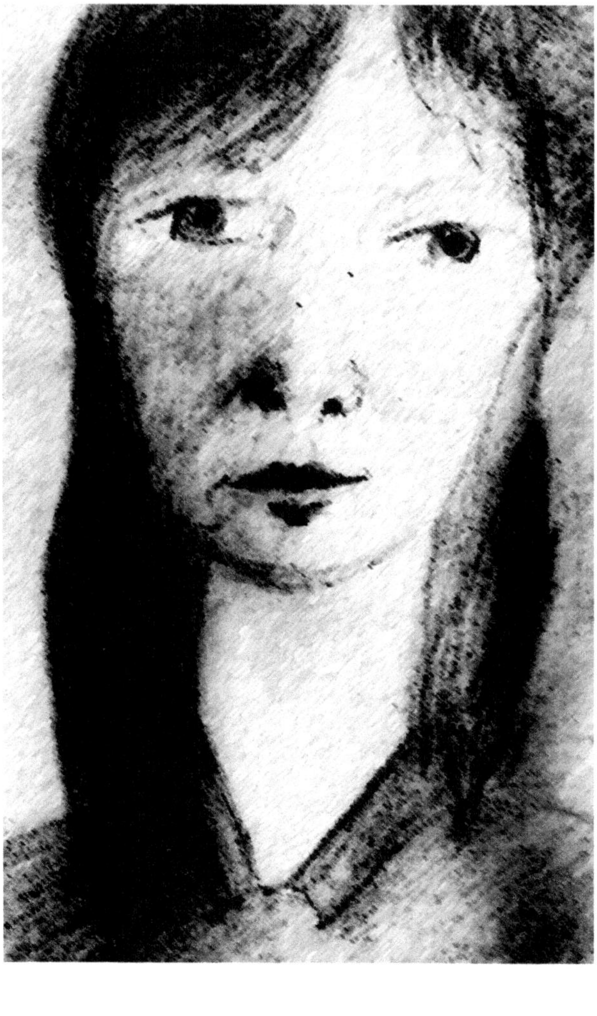

# Rebecca

The village had been there for many years and consisted of a circle of small houses, a school and the communal meeting hall. There were gardens and on one side of the village one could find the burial ground, which was devotedly maintained, as a place of peace and quiet where those who have moved on could be lovingly remembered. On the other side of the village there was the forest that always seemed so close and welcoming. Trees, flowers and the land all retained their own form of natural beauty within the changing cycle of seasons. There was no danger. People lived together in peace and harmony and all were descendents of those who had come from afar so many years ago. Life was gentle and uncomplicated.

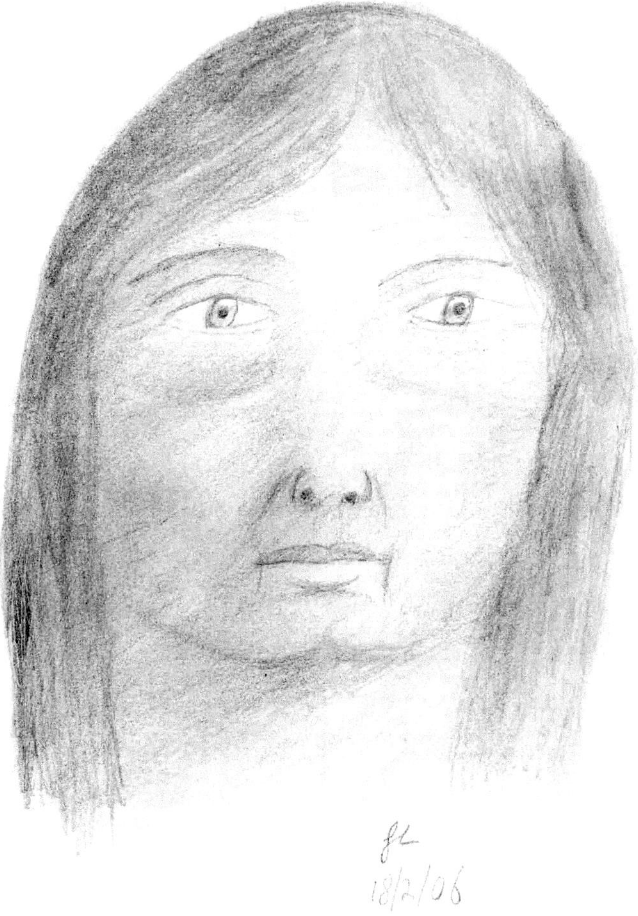
18/2/06

Adam was a fine, well-liked young man, With his sister, parents and grandparents he lived in a house on the edge of the village. By day and in all weathers they worked on the land coming together in the evening for a meal and to relax. Rebecca was a little younger than Adam who known as a lovely, caring person and was treasured by her family and all who knew her.

Adam and his parents often attended communal gatherings in the evenings that could consist of, among other items, musical evenings, poetry readings, discussions and many other things. Rebecca had a distinctly solitary and quiet side to her nature, she loved silence and being able to wander in the forest on fine days.

"Don't be away for too long" her concerned mother would say.

At times Adam and her father would echo those sentiments yet, Grandmother often told them –

"She is fine, trust the wise ones, our very dear Rebecca knows where she is going."

There were, among the villagers, those gifted with profound spiritual wisdom and insight. They were counsellors who had an all knowing and sensitive understandings of the way things are. Rebecca was very close to her Grannie. They would often sit and talk together as they were one afternoon in late autumn when trees     have their leaves into nature's hands for the carpeting of the forest.

A community gathering had claimed the attendance of the others.

They sat quietly together in the candle lit main room of the house. Grannie held a book in her thin old hands. It was one Rebecca had often seen her reading or just holding during periods of silence and deep thought.

"Gran, can we talk please?"

"Of course my dear one, you know I am always hear for you."

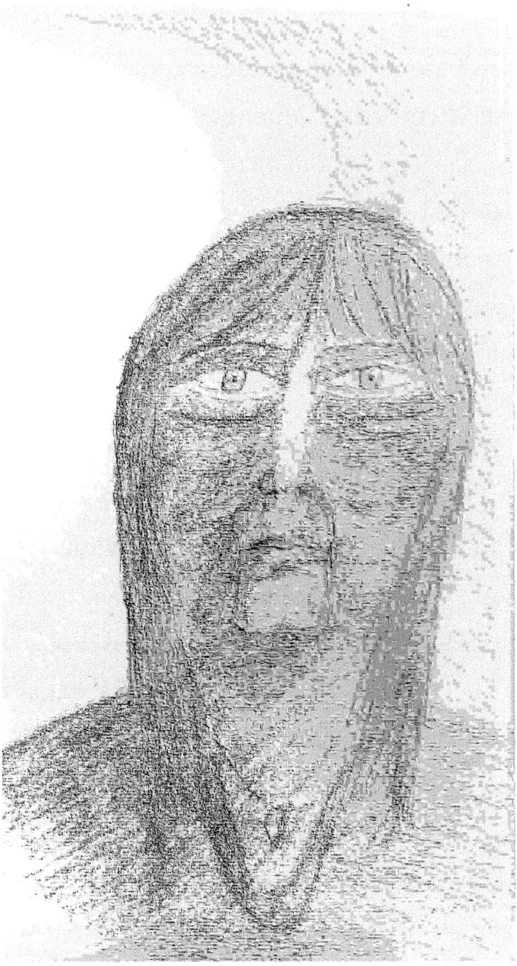

*John and Other Stories*

A gently warm fire glowed in the hearth where the flames, tongues of quiet fire, glanced and crackled.

"I walked in the forest today, there was a wonderful quiet with trees seeming to reach upward for meaning and truth"

Firelight illumined the face of the old one who had such deep and piercing brown eyes.

"This was something you felt?" she asked smiling quietly

"It was, yes, I seemed to feel it in such a close, near way and, walking softly on the leaves I had a sense of another presence."

"Dear Rebecca, golden child of nature it is a blessing to perceive with the heart as you have. This is the seeing and allowing of the presence of all life, and you saw today that you are part of the one life which in all its variations is held by the holiness of purity."

Rebecca sat at her Granny's feet and, reaching up, touched her hand.

"You have such wonderful understanding," she said

"Wisdom my child, resides in comfort in all that is simple. I knew I would be among the wise ones at an early age as I saw more and more with my spirit. So much that we know and feel is essential is also unseen. I too loved nature and will, at the appropriate time return from nature from whence I came. In the warmer seasons sunshine streams gently through branches leaving lovely patches of light where we walk. So, my dear Rebecca, forests in the mind allow patches of light, life is the seeking for the clearing where all is light, beauty and truth."

"Please tell me about the book."

With a sense of reverence Grannie took Rebecca's face in her hands and kissed her forehead.

"Bless you," she said, "You are so deeply precious and always will be and yes, you will find all you seek. Within the pages of this book Rebecca are the teachings and experiences of wise ones from many years past. All wise ones have one and The Counsellor Of The Wise gives it to them"

"Where does he live?"

"Away on the farthest edge of the forest."

"How long has he been there?

"Well, nobody knows but it would be for many generations. Actually, I can well remember asking my own Grandmother the very same question."

The room was gently warm. Opening the book she sat back and began reading in the friendly glow of candle -light.

"Listen to the rivers of wind flowing through the trees, feel the cool air of the forest scented with flowers, grass and the loving abundance of nature, be truly in the moment and know that you and the wonders of nature around you are but different manifestations of the one life. Wisdom is a lost, innocent child seeking to find refuge in those who will love her and allow her light to shine through them to others."

The old one paused, turned a page then began reading again.

"Light and shadow walk together on the human pathway, in shadow look for light, it is so near yet perhaps obscured by shadows within oneself. Find always light within, light that grows in silence and in yearning for true wisdom. Shadows will leave yet must be allowed to go. Look for light, be aware of light radiated often from the unexpected scource. All life flows to one-ness, to peace, joy indeed will come in the morning, in the valley of the shadow is the true light, seek always the way of light and love and all in the healing fullness of time will indeed be well.

"Who wrote that?" Rebecca asked.

"A wise one many years ago yet, wisdom and truth flow from many different sources and the holy light of innocence allows the mind to be open and receptive."

"The words touched me"

"They will, true wisdom will always resonate within your whole person for I can see a golden light all around you and soon, even now, you will journey forth to seek the Counsellor Of The Wise."

"Will I?"

"Indeed you will, this is certain"

"What will the others say?"

"Go with all our love"

"And our blessing"

"And know that love in truth will never pass away."

Three voices she knew gently entered the atmosphere of the candle-lit room. Rebecca turned and smiled. Standing behind her were her parents and Adam who spoke about their shared experience of compulsion to return early, something drew them.

After warmly embracing Rebecca they joined her at the old one's feet. Still the lovely log fire glowed and touched them with its gentle warmth. Flames, tongues of quiet fire danced as if with a gentle joy.

"Indeed love in truth will never pass away. My dear husband, your Grandfather Rebecca, returned to nature before you were born as, before long, will I yet, love will link us now and always."

A gathering quietness, no real need to speak as between them flowed a silent communion of love that one saw and felt with the heart. Then, addressing the whole family, the old one continued –

"Always pray my dear ones, prayer will link you with the divine help, love and caring are always there waiting for you to reach out. Angels, clear seeing wise friends are all around you, allow yourself to see them and to feel them, this is recorded in the higher annals of the wise ones."

"How do you feel darling?" Rebecca's mother asked

"Very happy, and ready to go forth to follow the precious calling of my destiny."

"The time dear one is, indeed now. Come to me my child."

Rebecca came and, with a sense of reverence, the old one placed her hands on her head.

"Go now, blessed child of spiritual light. Go along the path ordained for you in the times of the old ways. Go with the true blessing of all divinity and know love and prayers go with you on every step of your way. Tread soft, as a leaf, with a pure heart and quiet mind and in the fullness of time all will be well."

A moment of silence. Rebecca embraced all of her family then slowly walked out into the close and welcoming evening.

It was late afternoon. The sky was slowly darkening and stars were points of light enriching the sky. There was a full moon that seemed to bathe the path with its innocent light. Rebecca was in deep thought as she walked along. Within her heart sang a prayer for the family and friends who she loved so much. The growing night seemed to bring with it a keen sense of anticipation. The edge of the forest, looking upward tall trees seemed to touch the sky. A path lined with shadows lay ahead. For a moment Rebecca felt anxious.

"Welcome" a voice said "There is nothing for you to fear dear friend, no, nothing at all."

The voice was kind and had a lovely comforting quality that Rebecca could feel; she looked around yet nobody was visible.

"Thankyou for your welcome. Where are you?"

"You can see us"

"Us?"

"Yes, shadows are all along your path as they are on all paths. I am the voice of the shadows."

Rebecca felt much calmer now. All along the moonlit path she could see many shadows as well as a light glowing in the distance.

"We are teachers and friends" the voice said "Light and shadow populate every human path, they are an element that is built into your existence itself. Allow us to share our teaching and to be your true friends and we will guide you to the light of the deeper wisdom."

"I understand"

Rebecca sat down to rest for a few moments. The grass was clean and fresh and her searching gaze found many flowers with their petals closed in sleep.

"Your path will be one of learning, growth and joy. You have been chosen to join the company of the wise ones and a time will come when truly you will be a blessing to many."

"Thankyou"

"Rise now beloved and go on your way. Before too long you will come to a clearing and a wise friend will meet you there."

Rebecca felt calm and happy; she got up and continued her journey. There was a lovely sense of peace within the forest. Every so often different birds would sprinkle the air with song and, she was noticing trees, flowers and the grass wearing drops of recently fallen rain like glittering jewels yet, she recalled that there has actually been no rain for three days.

All long her journey Rebecca was finding out how precious each and every moment of life could be. Raindrops glowed with light and each moment could be illumined with light, love and truth. The shadows were indeed friends and teachers who she could trust. There seemed to be no distinct sense of time. Before long she came to a clearing. It was illumined with gently glowing moonlight and there was even a seat for Rebecca to pause and enjoy a needed rest.

A lone Gull called across the darkening sky then, with outstretched wings, glided quietly to the ground and settled in front of her. The only area of sea that Rebecca knew of was several miles away yet one lone Gull had come a long way inland. Rebecca closed then opened her eyes. Before her was a beautiful young girl with long, gleaming blond hair who wore a golden dress and silver robe. For a moment the air seemed to be full of the piercing cries of Gulls then, a silence.

"Hello Rebecca" said the girl smiling.

"You know me?"

"Yes, we all do"

"All?"

"Yes, all us from the world of light and truth and some of us will be waiting on your path. It is a path your dear Grandmother trod and was blessed with pure wisdom and light. Here, in this clearing there is rest and precious space for you and space is so very important."

Rebecca watched as the girl approached holding in her young hands a book and a pink rose; she appeared to be a little younger than Rebecca and had gentle blue eyes.

"My name is Nardinia," she said quietly

"That was Granny's name"

"Yes, that's right" she sat next to Rebecca "I am the spirit of your Grannie as a young girl and, I have been sent here to offer you these."

"Sent by who?"

"All questions will find their answers" Nardinia said smiling "There is no need for time here, this far into the forest and, special moments can be preserved for ever."

"Where?"

"In the temple standing within stillness in the secret places of the heart."

Nardinia's voice was soft and quiet.

"You have been called to walk the path of wisdom and knowledge Rebecca. Take the book and open it."

Rebecca carefully opened the book and turned its pages.

"There's nothing written"

"No, not yet. The book is indeed a sacred book. It is the book of your life and the empty pages are waiting for you."

"For me?"

"Yes, and you ought to try and turn just one page at a time. Remember too Rebecca that all life consists in differing manifestations and experiences of the one holy life of creation."

"And the rose?"

"The rose is that one life with petals forever open to light. It has such beauty yet also thorns. Hardness and softness. Light and shadow. All walk side by side throughout existence and all, in their way are teachers. This is simple wisdom for you to hold, carefully, as you hold the book and the rose. You can write in the book as you feel led to and please always turn the pages one at a time.         . Very often a person can try and turn too many pages, which only leads to seeing and learning little if anything. You will receive peace, love and the fullness of divine wisdom. You will understand the truth of the oneness of all time and creation and be able to share this with others."

"As Grannie and the wise ones do?"

"Yes"

"Nardinia closed her eyes and spent some moments in a deep silence before opening them

"Another is joining us," she said

Soon, the clearing was flooded in the most beautiful, glowing golden light that Rebecca had ever seen. Trees and everywhere she looked became verdant with the many differing colours of nature and the air was filled with the gentle chanting of beautiful, unearthly voices. Rebecca smiled, she felt calmly warm. Holding her hand Nardinia asked Rebecca to close her eyes.

A few moments passed. Rebecca opened her eyes and saw a man standing motionless in the centre of the clearing; he was tall and dressed in a deep blue robe and had shoulder length pure white hair. Rebecca noticed also that, in either hand, he held what seemed to be a crystal.

The man had a gentle feeling of wisdom and kindness about him.

"Dear Rebecca, now you can rest" his voice was deep and calm "I have come from the sacred realms of the holy life to offer you my blessing."

"Who are you?"

"It matters not, names are only words and I come to you from beyond anything that words can describe. From another dimension of ultimate reality. Rest is so important for you now."

Rebecca lay down placing her head on Nardinia's lap.

"That's right" Nardinia told her gently stroking her forehead.

Slowly, and with reverence the man raised both of his hands. A deep shining blue light emanated from the crystals to Rebecca, he began chanting in a solemn and low voice-

"May you know the divine abiding, the friendship of spiritual wisdom and the light of truth and knowledge. May understandings of the way things are always give you clear sight. May you learn to live fully in each moment of time reaching always for true love that is eternal and will soothe away all fear. May you find the joy of your true self and be at peace. For all things dear child of eternity, there is an appointed time."

Rebecca drifted safely into sleep, The pause for rest was truly needed and it was some time before two gently cool drops of water touched her eyes: she woke and stood up. Now, there was nobody at all in the clearing. Feeling refreshed and joyful Rebecca continued on her journey holding the book and the rose.

The path seemed very long yet, she was glad to tread it. Cool air touched her face like caring hands bringing memories of how both her Mother and Grandmother would, at times hold her face in their hands as they also did with her brother. It was a lovely feeling of being valued and precious

As Rebecca continued thoughtfully along the sky passed from night to early morning. Near, far birds gave voice to their joy within the created order; their songs fell gently into the quietness. Still the shadows but now they were all the more welcome as kind friends.

"Pause and rest awhile" said the voice of shadows "You are making very good progress indeed."

"Am I?"

"Yes, without any doubt and in every way you are growing and learning. The wise can always become wiser"

Again Rebecca was glad of some rest and a chance to enjoy the gathering stillness. Looking into all the shadows and darkness ahead she saw, in outline what seemed to be a group of people."

"Hello" she called

No reply. They all remained motionless.

"Rebecca, it us " said the voice "Once we were strangers…"

"But not now" said Rebecca "Far from it"

"That's right, and there are many different kinds of strangers."

Rebecca listened intently as wonderful wisdom and insight came from this quiet voice.

"Where Rebecca, is the holy quiet of strangers? In space around you. In stillness and seeking after wisdom and knowledge. A quiet and wise stranger will only come when invited and will give to others a truly great gift…"

"That of silence and space" said Rebecca

"Yes, and in this space one can feel the soothing vibrations of eternity opening the way to wise ones, to clear seeing angels. Allow time for you and allow those with gently quiet vibrations to come giving honour, respect and love. In locating your calling you will find peace with yourself."

"There is a door to peace with you" another voice called. A man and woman were walking slowly toward them.

"The handle is on the inside" the new voice continued, "Love, light, joy, wisdom and the gift of giving and receiving healing are on the outside, only you yourself may welcome them in."

Rebecca got up and began to walk toward them. A joyful smile lit her face and she ran with outstretched arms. The woman was her Grandmother. They held each other very close while the man smiled and looked on.

"Grannie, its so lovely to see you"

"Lovely to see you as well darling, bless you"

Grannie gently touched her head then turning to the man asked-

"Do you know who this is?"

Rebecca looked at the man and smiled, like Grannie he too wore a long gleaming white garment. There was a feeling, something familiar about the man, something that said he was wise, kind and belonged to that place at that time. Rebecca smiled, she knew him.

"Yes, I do, hello Granddad"

They embraced. A lovely quietness moved between the three of them. Rebecca noticed her own garments were now gleaming white.

"Why?"

"White robes are the garments of the wise," said Granddad

"And I have come here" began Grannie "Because my appointed time had come. There is, every day ordinary time and an appointed time when a person reaches a special spiritual time in their existence and, my time to enter the higher life had come."

"Grannie how's Mum and Dad and dear Adam?"

"Fine and coping very well. They understand that we are still very close. There is no real seperation. Love in truth never dies and will link us and all of the one life forever. Do you like your white robe darling?"

"Yes, its so lovely"

"Consider Rebecca, what great peace may be found in white" said Granddad "It is a symbol of purity holding within it all the wonderful colours of the rainbow. Return to purity always, this is the home of your true self. One of the treasures so many need to find is a pure love, that is always in reverence and in truth. It will gently lead to compassionate service and self-giving and yourself being made moment by moment into the image of the divine."

"What exactly is this image of the divine?"

"It is yourself darling learning, growing and being true to the true you" Grannie replied quietly "All can be restored. Those who seek wisdom will, be sure, find wisdom and the deep joy of a pure heart and a quiet mind. So, dear Rebecca, consider white and all the healing and gladness found in the colours of the rainbow arching the sky and calling you to return to your true self."

"Is it time to go on?"

Grannie smiled and nodded.

"We are now in a life where there is no concept of time" she went on "We can be, now, as we remember each other to be. We are all blessed children of the Father who created the one life, Before we journey on let us realise that in time,

Rebecca, you will come back to this point as a wise one. Let us enter quietness and wait for a few moments, I know a prayer will be given to you."

Silence, deep and vast then Rebecca began –

"Our precious Father, dwelling in light beyond light, here, in the glory of your created order be near to me. God eternal mother, father holy one take me on, show me the path of the peacemaker, help me to know and to take the first step, which is peace with myself. May I embrace life as a Gull with outstretched wings floats, hovers and embraces each moment it is close to the heart of nature. May I call across vastness knowing my voice is heard." As my path reveals pastures new may I be ever mindful of treasures along the way. May I seek a wise heart and a quiet mind and may I live in truth and purity.

Another gathering silence before they continued their journey. The forest was beautiful now. Tall noble trees arched overhead and through their branches pools of light illumined the onward path. Birds sang with joy and occasional squirrels, deer and even dogs and cats ran before them. Granddad explained that there was no hunting. No killing of any kind in order to stay alive, no killing not only as in taking another's life or in cruel words and actions that will maim and destroy the wonder of the sensitive person. Rebecca sensed spiritual love all around and everywhere.

As they walked on other white robed figures joined them. Rebecca noticed none of them were carrying a book and a rose. Grannie smiled and explained that these were left with the Counsellor Of the Wise as symbols of the earnest desire to serve with all the holy gifts a person had been given. There were people she and her family had known who had undergone to journey to this life and others who had come especially to be with Rebecca.

"I'm so happy," said Grannie smiling

"And I" said Granddad

"Before long you will be received into our wise company" Grannie continued, "I can well remember that I was about your age when I first set out along this path."

"I know, and your spirit still lives on, we met earlier"

Increasing numbers of white robed figures appeared many of whom waved and smiled. Rebecca felt a keen sense of anticipation as Grannie explained that they were all from among the company of the wise from many centuries past. Some called out greetings which Rebecca joyfully returned

"After you have been ordained you will return" said Grannie "Notice the rose you carry, it still blooms in all its beauty, it is the one life itself in its glory of original innocence. Words are appearing and will continue to appear, words of wise comfort and teaching that you will pass on to others. So much depends on peace with you.

Rebecca smiled. The sky was gently darkening and the forest became illumined with new moonlight.

"Where are the glories of creation?" Grannie asked "Around you, above you, beneath you and also within you. Spiritual beauty dear one is born from peace within yourself. Peace may be gently embraced in stillness, and being within each moment as you live one moment at a time. The present moment is where you will find yourself. Find the precious the precious light of the one life that is truth embodied within you."

Rebecca closed her eyes listening intently as the words resonated within her. Granddad quietly rejoined them.

"The one you are in truth will be at peace and discern all forms of untruth and deception. Be still like a tree whose verdant branches will move in all the winds of creation yet, in time, return to stillness. This is the way of holiness, the way of the true and wise heart. My dear one peace has, as a lost and frightened child seeking safety and love. Receive that child in the purity of the now and allow true peace with your true self."

"Come," said Granddad smiling "We must go on"

"Yes" said Rebecca "But look…"

A young girl in ragged and torn clothes walked toward them, she seemed very frightened and had clearly been crying.

"Can I speak with you Rebecca?" she asked

"Yes, of course"

"You are already so very wise and kind. I have come as the voice of all who seek inner harmony, purity and the joy of peace with themselves, please say a prayer for us

"Dear friend. There needs to be opening to ever present truth. As you are spirit walk in spirit and in truth. May you find the joy of your true self and know deep peace within yourself. Find your sanctuary within each moment of time, may you live safe and free from harm and, when you journey on, may you find treasured loved ones waiting and know loved ones left behind will always be bound to you and the created order in love that is in truth. May you be led into all truth and peace."

Rebecca opened her eye. The girl had gone. Slowly, they journeyed on the house of the Counsellor Of The Wise. Rebecca knew gentle inner joy and could sense the blessing in her companions and in all they met.

"What kind of home does he live in Grannie?"

"His home for today and for always links with his purpose and with true wisdom."

"For today...?

"Yes, his real home is the longing heart of all who seek a true way and the spiritual love at the heart of the one life. Among all the sick, the sorrowing and the desperately lonely he makes his home calling to them silently with gently outstretched arms. Always he is simple and uncomplicated."

Rebecca smiled; she understood deeply and well. Wisdom and truth are all around and ever present. The path they walked was leading to her destiny. The end would be a newly created beginning and in the end all would indeed be well. In the distance she saw everyone converging on a small cottage among flowers and trees.

"And what's his real name?"

"Darling, he has so many names and is knowable to all. We whose company you are joining have many names also; we are those taking messages of wisdom, love and truth to the farthest reaches of time and the universe. We are his messengers and some people call us angels."

As they arrived at the house the others were waiting outside.

The flowers outside were of every colour and aroma. Calm and a gathering peace enfolded the entire assembly.

"Welcome to my garden"

The voice was calm and soft seeming to carry a clear vibration of wisdom that resonated within Rebecca; she had no doubt who it was.

"Is not mortal life as a garden" he continued "At times I, the loving gardener will gather my flowers unto myself. Now, let us enter the moments that follow and nurture a lovely flower blooming among us. Welcome dear Rebecca."

"Thankyou" said Rebecca and bowed reverently with the gathered assembly.

"Where is a flowers true beauty?" he continued, "Where it meets the eye searching for wisdom and truth. There needs to be spaces for this sensitive awareness of the way things are. Where is the beauty of personhood? In receiving light as a flower does, with open gladness."

Bird song entered the calm, still air.

"Rain will bring refreshment and peace. On all pilgrim path
there will be joy and sorrow yet, notice raindrops on a flower glistening like precious jewels. True beauty is found in nature and is created from it. Beauty in nature, beauty of your true self. In time you will proceed on your journey toward life beyond life with quiet calm

and joy, embrace all occasions to grow open like a flower to the holy light of truth."

Silence.

"Rebecca, I welcome you, please come in with the others. Your Grandparents will be your guardian wise ones, please would you now give your Grandmother your book and rose and come as I await you with such profound joy in my heart."

They went into the house and entered a large, circular room. The walls were a deep blue and golden light streamed in through two circular windows and the glass canopy above. The entire assembly sat in a semi-circle around a single table draped with a white cloth. An old wooden chair stood on its far side. Behinds this were deep red curtains. Rebecca felt great joy as a man emerged, she felt who it was.

"I am so very honoured to welcome you Rebecca"

"Thankyou"

The man looked elderly, had long black hair with a moustache and long beard. Rebecca felt drawn to his kind and gentle eyes, she noticed his light blue robe with a silver sash around the middle. The room was hushed as he came to the table and closed his eyes.

"Consider a candle" he began after a while "Complete and whole in itself. Within its embrace are space and emptiness. Creation itself is complete, from life ones moves on to the higher life. All life is sacred and is encircled by holy and creative life energy. You too, my dear child, are sacred. All of your pilgrimage is a seeking after wholeness, for completition and in your seeking receive into the holy circle of your personhood all the compassion and insightful and insightful wisdom and knowledge you will find, we all honour and bless you now."

The counsellor and the entire assembly extended their hands. Rebecca felt her entire body filling with spiritual joy. Silence.

"Please consider what peace may be found in healing silence," he continued. This is a special silence one can allow to enter the depths of one's being. In stillness, seek the holy way of wisdom and truth; this way is among all that is calm and simple. Follow what we often call the way of the wise heart."

Again the special joy thrilled Rebecca's entire being.

"This is the heart that can touch others with deep compassion and truth and is, as well, a heart at peace with itself. What dear one, is your wise heart saying to you? If you listen in truth you will hear in truth and what you hear, sense and even see will carry the soft vibration of spiritual music. As you dwell in the light of spiritual purity, which is the light of your true self you will always walk in light truly dear one, I know."

Silence, he walked slowly and thoughtfully to the front of the table.

"Rebecca, do you remember the young one you spoke to on the way here?"

"Yes, do you know her?"

"Close your eyes and open them"

When Rebecca opened her eyes the girl stood, smiling, in front of her. Rebecca smiled and actually did not feel surprised to see her. As she grew in wisdom moment-by-moment understanding came of this life beyond the earthly dimension.

"Bless you Rebecca" she said "May you know through all eternity the blessing of spiritual wisdom and love. Do please close your eyes again."

As Rebecca opened her she found herself greeted by the vast and kind eyes of the counsellor.

"You!" she exclaimed quietly

"Yes indeed, you see, we have met before.

Smiling he slowly returned to the other side of the table.

"This is the altar of dedication, please come Rebecca and place your hands upon it. This is a time and place for the giving of yourself in true service and love. You will grow moment by moment in love, light and truth and take compassion to all of the areas your destiny will send you. Is this what you truly desire?"

"Yes, it is"

"Please join your hands with mine"

As their hands linked a glorious blue light glowed between them.

"This is the light of healing" he said "You have been given a gift to heal and the healing hands of the creator will always work through your hands, all manner of things will be well, all illness

distress and trouble will find an oasis of comfort and healing in you, do you truly desire this?"

"Yes, I do"

"My dear child you are now one of our assembly, we honour and truly welcome you. Go now to your Grandparents and see what Grannie has for you"

Rebecca ran to them, they embraced and Grannie gave Rebecca her own book of The Annals Of the Wise Ones. Others also showed Rebecca their love, loyalty and affection. Now she would walk the sacred way of the wise heart and teach this way to others.

The counsellor raised his hands. Silence.

"Blessed are those who walk in quietness, all their ways will be of clear understanding. Blessed is the true and noble friend, this friend is all of the spiritual life. Blessed is the holy power of gentleness, the quiet vibration when one is with a dear and loving soul. Blessed is the blade of grass that bows with the breeze yet always upward to the beyond and the infinite. Friends, dear ones, now spend time with each other and know that even though you may not see me I will always be among you."

Slowly, he turned and walked slowly back behind the curtain. There followed a time of talking and sharing after which the great assembly of the wise all went their separate ways. Rebecca and her Grandparents returned to the path that would take her back home.

"How long have I been away Grannie?"

"For as long as was needed. How do you feel darling?"

"Calm and so very happy"

"Good, I know that you will be a much loved wise one and you will be returning to a world where pure healing wisdom and insight are so much needed.

"That's right" said Granddad "In due time you will travel and wherever you go you will be an inspiration and blessing to many."

Birds sang as they entered the forest.

"We return to the thought that all life is one" Granddad continued, "The lovely birds are all part of that same one life and now, they rejoice with you as you have become a living temple of wisdom. For from you wisdom will cry and understanding speak with your voice."

They walked on and again they linked with their friends the shadows. Rebecca knew too, there are shadows within people that obscure the vision of divine reality accessible to every human soul. Soon they reached the edge of the forest. Rebecca's parents were there and she ran to their fond embrace then, turning saw her Grandparents had gone.

"Lets go home" said Adam

"Yes" said Rebecca "I've much to tell you and..." she smiled "Alot to do" They walked quietly away.

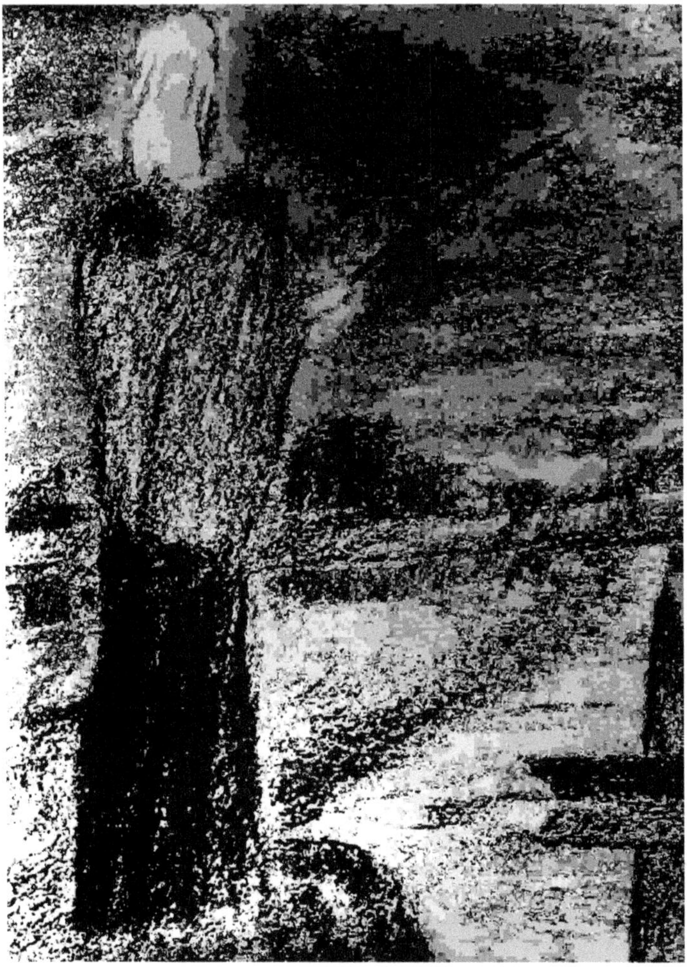

# Talking Together

Journey almost over. The young couple had been travelling for many days and gazed gladly at the hill overlooking a vast expanse of sea where an island was distantly visible. The man on the hill was wise and very kind, seeming to see clearly into people and touch them with his word while they conversed with him.

"My dear friends" he called "I have been expecting you"

A calm and bright day with a breeze touching their faces like a gentle hand.

"Expecting us?" echoed the young man curiously.

"Yes"

They approached the man and found him easy to talk to. There were no barriers. They stood together on the hill looking at the serene sea before them.

"I'm Rachel"

"I'm Declan"

"Welcome, tell me dear ones, tell me, why are you not at peace with yourselves."

"Well, we heard about you" began Rachel "We've come as our lives, our society and even our world are lost and in such pain."

"Perhaps the greatest pain is ignorance, not seeing clearly and not asking the right questions."

The man's voice was quiet and gentle; each tone carried a vibration of safety and peace.

"There's no justice," said Declan

"None anywhere" Rachel added as a tear trickled down her lovely young face "It's all so unfair, I'm frightened."

"I do understand" said the man calmly "This raises questions vast like the sea yet, as one looks across…

"…There's a distant island, the other shore," said Declan

"In all questions, indeed within the very word itself is there not the suggestion of a quest, a journey, so come let us reason and journey together."

"There is so much pain" Declan told him "Pain and there is no space to express hurt."

"Nobody to tell, nobody actually wanting to know, wanting to feel the agony of another."

"I understand" said the man "Feeling is truly important. Compassion is being able to share another's suffering and lead to healing and peace."

"I have known pain" said Declan "The pain none want to see, I've felt betrayed."

Rachel placed her arm lovingly around him; the man indicated a seat and they all rested together.

"Truly, you are Declan the truth seeker, I know what has happened to you."

Silence. How could the man know?

"Dear friends, do not be afraid that I know. My eyes see so very much. It was betrayal that led to you trying to end your life. Then, a gift from the divine…" he smiled at Rachel "Now, you are glad to be alive."

"Yes, I am"

"And you serve others in so many ways" Rachel told him

"True, Declan with Rachel your divine gift you seek and truly you shall find."

Gulls hovered overhead sending their piercing cries into eternity.

"Friends, there is the need for harmony, completeness, being one as all life is truly differing manifestations of the one life. A need for peace within the self, to flourish like a young flower opening to light, not as a leaf tossed in all directions in the dark times of the year, fallen and frail."

Rachel and Declan listened intently. The words vibrated gently within them. Rachel and Declan looked at each other. A silent joy touched them, finding secret places in the self where joy longs to live forever. They felt glad the man was smiling.

"Who exactly are you? asked Declan"

"I have many names, a name is a word, a sound which, once spoken will not return. The person too can live a more abundant and joyful life."

"There are many questions" Rachel sighed

"Indeed, and my friends we need to clothe sounds with meaning."

"We are concerned for justice" Declan spoke with some anxiety

"And are there not many meanings given to this word?" the man asked "So often it is linked with revenge, justice in truth can never be that, also linked with ideas of fairness and equality yet these should be self evident within a society."

"Greed and selfishness obstruct this" said Rachel

"Also ignorance" added Declan

"Ignorance of the way things are, so many within your societal groupings deprive others of the gifts of creation that can bless the whole person. Fragmented people who are deprived of wholeness become so wounded and hurt. The whole concept of punishment is infected with hurting, indeed, does not hurting the hurt only create more hurt?"

"We've lost our way," sighed Declan, Rachel held his hand

"Truly friend, yes, justice is walking the path of the hurting, the wounded and particularly perhaps the isolated. Softly treading the path seeking wisdom and clear seeing."

"Are these not gifts" Rachel asked

"They are, yes, and you Rachel the divine gift are caring for Declan the truth seeker."

The man paused, a lovely gathering silence came to them before he continued

"So, justice is treading the pained path of others, a pain that screams with many voices. Walking, is something you do as, is justice and it involves waling humbly and loving mercy. Dear truth seeker, divine gift may you always walk humbly, love mercy and know peace with yourselves. True justice from the person truly at peace with themselves."

"What passes for justice is so often corrupted by cruelty, furthering the interests of the selfish and vindictive and hurting those hurt already." Declan spoke thoughtfully. Those conflicting with false justice sometimes are labelled criminals."

"But who are the real criminals?"

"An important question Rachel" said the man "Should not true justice flow through the whole person and the whole society?"

"I wonder" began Declan "How much false justice links with lack of understanding of loss."

"Loss of what?" Rachel asked

"Loss of knowing one is precious now, loss of one's deserved and equal share in the goods of creation, loss of a loved person in one way or another."

"I'm sure you're right" said the man "If wholeness and unity within and among link with justice it must be the true justice we seek together, not the false abomination permeating human life at present

"So much links with loss" Declan sighed

"Very true" Rachel told him "Loss and pain where a person cannot feel their true worth, no sense of being precious, I feel this and my heart is so heavy."

"You both have deep wisdom" the man said "We are talking about hearing the scream of the hurt, feeling the desperation of the isolated – there is the need for profound clear sighted wisdom and understanding rather than the base and ignorant motivation of revenge. Each must share equally in the goods and blessings of the created order. Justice, like many concepts raises hard questions yet a wise man long ago talked about doing justice, loving mercy and walking humbly – these are three gifts with which to adorn the path of the hurt and isolated – mercy and humility are true companions of real justice and they must lovingly embrace wisdom who is the lost one in your world always asking 'why?'"

"Thankyou" said Declan. The man raised his hands

"The blessing of unending light and divine wisdom abide in you and flow through you always dear truth seeker, dear divine gift. May you be as one now and forever. Let us part in joy and peace."  The young couple walked away.

The man returned to the hill gazing out to the other shore.

# Prison

Silence between them. Each alone in a particular way. The lack of sound was hostile and menacing. One wore wrist manacles. Symbols of fear yet who, in truth, was afraid of what? Where is the real scource of the terror that linked them together? Manacles were also symbols of power, which, when rampant always leaves questions like, who are the real criminals?

There was time to think. The prisoner needed this. Always the looking. The prisoner also had many questions. Asking questions perhaps caused the real criminals most anxiety. Yet, things were just not right. A cold, barren room awaited him. The heavy door closed. Had light on his darkness come? It had not. Though frightened of his darkness the light that would illumine and disperse it frightened them so much more.

Sometimes sounds of others. Calling and desperate voices. Footsteps. The spy hole opens. Eyes look in. Again, of what are they afraid? It was a question wandering like a lost, phantom child. Times of a strange silence. Not where he could close his eyes and enter to find stillness and peace. It was a particularly sinister silence. One where there was no searching, worse, no listening. No wisdom and clear seeing.

Suicide in, or shortly after custody of one kind or another was very commonplace. Why no questions about this? No belt around his trousers in case he hung himself, no books and some other silly measures. The prisoner could see and feel why self-destruction in these circumstances was something of inevitability. No regard ever for the slow death inside. For a moment his closed his eyes. A presence. Opening them he saw a girl in a long blue gown.

"I know your torment within" she told him quietly "I can see it"

"Who are you?" he asked

"I am the wisdom you seek."

Silence between them. The prisoner sensed that this was a different lack of sound. Welcoming, kind and gathering

"There are many kinds of prison cell. I am kept in one that is fashioned by self – interest, inequality, cruelty and ignorance. All so very prevalent in your society particularly among those holding a corrupt power."

"Why have you come? He asked

"I have come as a young person. In youth and in innocence one can so often see and even experience the truth. Now, at this time I know you are in need of understanding and compassion. Dear friend, you are precious in the sight of God now."

"Am I?"

"Indeed you are" she continued, "A prison has formed within you. A main building block and support for it has been loneliness. Isolation. This is often so. Fear of being vulnerable to more and more hurts. Clear seeing truth is the only key."

Again, a silence that seemed to gather them. An eye looked in then he heard departing footsteps.

"I am come to you with a message of healing and of hope. There can be a peace within you. Release from the prison. Real peace with yourself. Truly, you are so precious in the sight of God. Take hold of the hand he offers now for his wonderful love is true and everlasting."

"Thankyou so much" said the prisoner with tears of deep relief in his eyes. A sense of calm and joy. Wisdom came forward and touched his head in a gesture of anointing. "God bless you" she said, "Take hold of real freedom" "I will" he told her and quietly fell asleep.

# The Old House

Morning. Light came to the old house. Slowly opening his eyes, he looked around. No sound. Easing back the covers the man got out of bed; he looked out of the window. Outside all was still and quiet. Nobody around. Too early even for the monotonous hum of the milkman's van and the chink of milk bottles on stone steps.

The man washed, shaved and got dressed. He felt quite well in himself. When he felt ready he slowly descended the stairs. He felt each step as it creaked in the silence. Once, there were people he loved. Now, they were missed. Part of him was gone yet; he knew that love indeed never dies. Love in truth would always link them.

A room. Turning the polished brass handle he entered. Bright, swirling lights greeted him. All the colours of the rainbow everywhere. A bed. Various toys. The sound of happy laughter.

"Welcome"

"Thankyou" he responded. It was a young girl's voice, "Where are you? He asked.

"I am where I need to be," said the girl

"I don't understand"

*George Coombs*

"You will" she told him "In this room is the innocence of childhood. All the longing to grow toward light and peace."

The man warmed to the voice. It held a lovely, safe vibration. Here was a precious place of refuge. He smiled.

"Go for now" she said, "Soon, I promise you will know."

He withdrew from the room quietly closing the door behind him. After a moments pause he descended another flight of stairs. Another room awaited him. Cold. A strange, sinister chill. The man did not want to enter yet; there was a sense that he must. It was vital for him. The door was stiff. A little force then entry was possible. All around darkness faintly illumined by a single candle. Again a voice –

"Come" it said

This was a harsh masculine tone. Shadows everywhere. One tall and fairly bright candle. Soon his eyes were comfortable with the dark and the shadow

"This is dark," said the voice "Shadows are all around you. So very often you go toward them. You even welcome and embrace them and allow them to embrace you.

"I know," he said, "So very often darkness can seem like light. It honestly can."

Desperation vibrated in his tone and every word.

"I do understand" said the voice "Look at the candle again."

"This is dark," said the voice "Shadows are all around you. So very often you go toward them. You even welcome and embrace them and allow them to embrace you.

"I know," he said, "So very often darkness can seem like light. It honestly can." Desperation vibrated in his tone and every word.

"I do understand" said the voice "Look at the candle again."

Beside the candle a smaller candle which the man was told to pick up. Gazing into the delicate flame he felt at peace.

"This is the light of truth," said the voice, "Take it, and allow its clear flame to lead you forth from darkness."

The man did as he was asked. Descending a final flight of stairs he found the main room of the old house. Still the stairs creaked but in a different way. As if calling out in pain. This room glowed in blue light. There was a table draped with a white cloth and a chair in which a woman sat quietly. A very young girl was also there.

"Come in" said the girl "Yes, it's me"

The man linked at once with the voice. He had heard it before in the first room.

"I am Truth Seeker" replied the girl who wore a long white robe and had shoulder length golden hair "We wish you well."

The woman in the chair was silent. A baby nestled in her arms. Looking carefully he saw she was clothed with a blue robe that was a somehow deeper blue than that in the room generally. The baby opened its wide and beautiful eyes. They held a distant and rather sad gaze.

"He looks away" said Truth Seeker "There is a great burden he will one day be called to carry yet, always he will love others so very deeply."

"Even me?"

Truth Seeker smiled

"Yes, of course" she said, "Even you and even now he loves you and wants to give you wonderful gifts."

The man was touched. Love being shown to him. A tear trickled down his cheek. It was so very wonderful. A lovely gathering safety.

"The two rooms" Truth Seeker continued, "Are you, your light, innocent side and your dark side. All people have these sides. You, my friend, can embrace light and innocence and move on from darkness. In the dark room the larger candle gave you gave you another candle that glowed with its light. This light brings healing and wholeness and is for you to take from the dark house to others.

The man listened intently.

"In the past you have been held back " she went on "Now you must come to light and be a scource of light"

"But who exactly are you?"

Seeker smiled. A lovely glowing expression adorned her young face. Music for his eyes.

"I have been with you always" she said, "I am the you that is deep within you dear friend. The house is the you that longs to be filled with love and light."

"Come to the light of my son." It was the woman who spoke; he voice carried a lovely, kind vibration.

The man sat with his precious young friend who handed him a gift wrapped in blue paper.

"What's this?" he asked

"Peace with yourself."

Closing his eyes the man rested. When he awoke the door of the house had been opened. Slowly, he walked to the welcoming light…

# The Stranger

Nobody knew where he was. Nobody cared. The man was away and alone. Before him, the sea lay vast and calm in the autumn light. A passing breeze gently touched his face and disturbed the grass. He paused. Always, he had loved nature. Grass bowed and swayed in all weathers. It knew shadows and light. At times it would glisten, jewel – like as with morning dew. Always vulnerable yet not broken while it had life. This is the way of gentleness.

Still he wandered. Gull cries filled the vast sky. All around him, presence of life in varying forms and movements. He was dead inside. The man could feel the beckoning of the ground below. He was very nervous. A sturdy fence lined the cliff edge. It would not stop him. The grass again. People could destroy grass by tearing and cutting at its roots with cruel hands. Destroying a beauty of nature. Rendering it worthless.

In this sense the man felt like the grass. To destroy himself. This was the only answer. He had known betrayal, Known and felt being betrayed, torn, lost and worthless. There was a fear. A terror of the ignorance that had been so wickedly insensitive to his many cries for help. Ignorance had abused him and driven him closer to the edge. He wept inside.

At times, he could think of others. They would miss him, maybe? Yet, how would he be received if they ever knew the truth? His mind was broken. Vision, thought were pained and broken into fragments. Then, he saw his shadow. Again, feeling of a call to kill himself. Death would be a welcome friend. He was a sensitive man who lived so much by feeling, intuition and insight.

Another look outward. He stood still. The time came closer and closer. Soon, there would be the end of all loneliness and all fear. Then, he saw another man in front of him. Who was he? A welcome stranger who cared and had a lovely quietness about him.

"Who are you?" the man asked

The stranger gently extended his hand. It was wounded, as was his other one. Wounds also in his side and around his head. The man went to him. The stranger was a man it was safe to be with.

"Who are you?" he asked again

"I was also wounded, pained" he said "I have called you as you are precious in my sight." He smiled, "I call you friend."

The man knew the stranger and loved him. They walked together in all the dark shadows. There was a way. There was truth. The stranger too had known and felt betrayed. Yet, he returned from death. Truly, the man knew who the stranger was.

Still the Gulls. They cried, swooped and soared. They were a choir in nature hymning the glories of creation. The stranger and the man walked away together. The man came to meet others. Friends of the stranger. There was a way and a true light. Shadows were also there yet the man could always find his companion from that day on the cliff. No longer a stranger, more a friend who stayed beside him in truth forever.

# The Park

He was by himself. Nobody had or would ever truly understand. John so often sought solitude. Who actually wanted to understand? So much pain and hurt, he was damaged inside. In human existence and interaction one is, always vulnerable. John knew this; he was a creative, sensitive and intelligent man. By profession, an academic with an engagement in many areas of knowledge. John was always seeking truth also, he knew, he wanted love. Nothing false or shallow but that which was real and would set him free. John needed peace with himself.

For many years he had cared for his wheelchair-disabled mother. They became very close; her body was devastated with arthritis, often they shared in the pain and distress. Fortunately John had skills and knowledge that had helped her a good deal, he was particularly skilled with his hands. They became travelling companions and very special friends. John loved her so much.

It was autumn. A very special time of year which would often find John wandering in the park near where he lived. Carpets of fallen leaves lay everywhere. Near naked trees seemed to reach out with a sense of yearning. He sat on a bench.

In quiet memory Mum came. Always the courage, the wonderful smile and concern for others. They were so very close. Laughing and weeping together. Sharing joy and so very much pain and desperation. Gulls flew across the sky filling its vastness with their mournful cries. Thoughts and memories crowded his mind. Words that people spoke following Mum's passing. Words can be so deeply hurtful and wounding.

"Well, you must let her go and move on."

"I know how you feel"

"Is your Mum dead? You're joking?"

John remembered; he was thankful for others who had journeyed with him affording space to talk or weep as much or as little as he wished. It was not a matter of getting over it in due time. It would take as long as it would take.

Their living room held special memories. They enjoyed breakfast there in the early mornings. John carried out treatment with skill, respect and sensitivity. Sometimes they listened to the radio and often Tinkle their little grey cat joined them.

"So good you're here dear" Mum often said.

The fact of being there mattered so much. Mum had passed on and there had been a particular death inside him. John had known grieving. There had been a serious suicide attempt but he was able to survive. Mum helped. John realised that on the day of her funeral his presence there was of great importance. Just for a moment he closed his eyes.

"Is everything alright dear"

A middle-aged woman walking her small dog stood before him.

"Only you looked so sad"

"I'm alright thankyou" John told her a little resentfully.

"Are you sure?"

"Yes. I am"

The woman had intruded. It was his time. John hated this; he wanted and valued his time and space. The woman was in no way welcome. John walked away. There were other paths. Dry, dead leaves everywhere

A cool breeze touched his face. Again, a memory. Mum always had a lovely way of holding John's face in her hands. This park was a place she loved and he had loved since early boyhood. Seasons changed and John knew that even to exist was to change, grow and continually seek for meaning and purpose. Another seat. A solitary man sat at one end, John sat away from him.

Neither disturbed the other. This stranger allowed John his space. Half an hour passed before the man quietly spoke –

"It's a blessing to be alone sometimes," he said

John was glad of the man; he sensed a gentle wisdom with him. The man was elderly and looked oriental. John agreed and went on –

"I love this park"

"Good" said the man "You miss someone so very much"

The man turned and bowed slightly.

"My mother" John told him

"I do understand. Well, love dear friend never dies. It is the shining eternal link between us and close ones who have journeyed a little way ahead."

People passed by oblivious of John and his companion. Still the Gull cries penetrated the vastness of nature like a searching question. John warmed to this man; he sensed genuine understanding and compassion.

"Think of the idea of resurrection." The man said, " In its Greek origin the word conveys the idea of standing again. All of creation, in the wisdom of God, is one. Love will always unite. Love in truth never dies."

"Yes, I can believe this" John told him

"Angels, wise ones are close. You will sense them."

He paused, a lovely gathering calm grew between them.

"Your spiritual senses convey that your loved ones are among them. A cloud of safety and love."

This was profound wisdom. It touched John as he absorbed it.

"Allow tears, and allow grieving. They will teach, comfort and enable you to go on. Truly, all in time will be well."

John felt better; he thanked the kind gentleman and asked –

"Where are you from?"

"China, from an ancient Chinese family but I have been here for some time. There is much to do. I have been honoured to be a companion on your journey."

"Thankyou" said John

Again change. Rain touched their faces. The man smiled.

"Perhaps we should part company " John said "Before it pours down."

"Alright. Rain can beautify a blade of grass and does not grass and does not grass teach us so much. It can be beautiful, receive light. It will bend and sway in all weathers but not break. So too tears can beautify and teach. One knows and will know forever love that makes life worth living.

"There's so much wisdom in nature" John declared thoughtfully.

"Indeed" the man agreed

"It's been good to meet you"

"You also" said the man bowing slightly

John turned, the rain gradually increased. Suddenly there came the realization that they had not exchanged names. He turned. The man had gone. John went back to his lodgings, had a meal and sat for a long time in deep thought.

# Again

Again, the fear and pain. Agony of isolation screaming where none chose to hear. Yes, closing his eyes he walked slowly along the path. Darkness close and threatening. Looking, searching he found the ruined castle. Nobody about. No sound as he approached and went in.

"Thankyou for coming" a voice said

"Who are you?"

"I am the voice from shadows. The boat that carries far away"

Looking through the oval windows he could just discern a boat with a tall sale moving slowly across a wide expanse of river.

"Why am I here?"

"To learn, to reflect and consider"

"Learn?"

"The castle is in ruins now. It has stood so for countless ages. Nobody has cared. Ruin has followed desertion and betrayal"

He listened intently.

"Friend, you have been as the castle"

"This s very true. I have longed to end a life blighted by hatred, isolation and betrayal."

*George Coombs*

"I know. Your feelings are the betrayal of humanity by itself. There needs to be clear seeing of the preciousness of every human soul and, dear one, you are so very precious."

"Am I?"

"Yes, you are, you have been a light shining in darkness for some time and the darkness has tried to consume you."

"But where am I?"

"It matters not as it is beyond words. It is another reality"

"A place to find"

He turned, through another window shone a delicate shaft of glowing, golden light. It was a young, quiet voice.

"I am the light of innocence and truth. I live in you as an angel with outstretched, holy hands longing to take you on."

"To be with me always?"

"Yes, I am the light arising from being still and knowing. Light and darkness walk along every human pathway. I am the light of wisdom and clear seeing."

As he watched the glowing, glorious form of an innocent child appeared before him. Slowly, she walked closer while glowing ever more brightly.

"Return now, I am always with you"

The man left the ruined castle and walked quietly away. It all came back to him, the cliff top, the tablets yet, also a vision of a future opening

his eyes. It was good to be alive. Yawning, he settled in his hospital bed and drifted into the loving arms of sleep.

# A Little About Me

I have had several different occupations in my lifetime. They range from clerk, grocer, shop worker, nurse then I entered higher education and engaged in my undergraduate and postgraduate studies and I am now a lecturer by profession. Yet, with all this I have always loved writing and felt a need to write, to put into words what I think, feel and know wanting, in so doing to enter into the reality of existence and share in a way that might help others during their pilgrimage through life to the waiting life to come.

Much about this can be difficult yet, immensely satisfying. Such themes as loss, isolation, suffering, death, longing have been companions on my own journey as they have, of course for many others. At one time I made up things from my imagination, now I write about what I feel, know and experience and in attempting this I try and use language in a way that is careful and sensitive.

A significant impetus toward my evolving into the writer I am today had been the passing of my mother. Mum was, for many years wheelchair disabled with arthritis and I was her carer and companion carrying out all her treatment, everything, you name it I did it all through those years. Many people, I know, join me in remembering Mum's courage, good humour and concern for others, Dad and I missed her very much then, just last year Dad also passed on. I have written much poetry arising from this one of which won an award and, I have been through periods of trial and distress myself which have set me thinking and producing the work I do now as a writer and artist.

I've often had a sense of a humanity that has lost its way and is functioning in a manner that is bound to produce despair and ever escalating stress levels. The hard questions that many people would acknowledge if given the chance are not being asked. There is a need to explore beneath the surface, to question the way things are, to seek for clarity in our concern for justice, love, truth, meaningful community, life, death and to ensure we have a real concern for wholeness and healing for ourselves and for others. May I wish peace to all who read this book.

George Coombs

Printed in Great Britain
by Amazon